Welcome to The Giggle Club

The Giggle Club is a new series of picture books made to put a giggle into early reading. There are funny stories about a contrary mouse, a dancing fox, a turtle with a trumpet, a pig with a ball, a hungry monster, a laughing lobster, an elephant who sneezes away the jungle, and lots more! Each of these characters is a member of **The Giggle Club**, but anyone can join: just pick up a **Giggle Club** book, read it, and get giggling!

Turn to the checklist on the inside back cover and check off the Giggle Club books you have read.

TEE-HEE!

HA-HA!

For Fergus

First U.S. paperback edition 1997

The Library of Congress has cataloged the hardcover edition as follows:

Jeram, Anita.
Daisy Dare / Anita Jeram.— 1st U.S. ed.
Summary: Daisy dares to do anything, but when her friends dare her
to take the bell off the sleeping cat, she hesitates.
ISBN 1-56402-645-0 (hardcover)
[1. Mice—Fiction. 2. Behavior—Fiction.]   I. Title.
PZ7.J467Dai   1995
[E]—dc20   95-6305

ISBN 1-56402-986-7 (paperback)

10 9 8 7 6 5 4 3 2 1

Printed in Hong Kong

This book was typeset in Columbus.
The pictures were done in watercolor and ink.

Candlewick Press
2067 Massachusetts Avenue
Cambridge, Massachusetts 02140

Anita Jeram

Daisy Dare

CANDLEWICK PRESS
CAMBRIDGE, MASSACHUSETTS

Daisy Dare did things
her friends were much
too scared to do.
"Just dare me," she said.
"Anything you want.
I'm never, *ever* scared!"

So they dared her to walk along the wall.

They dared her to eat a worm.

They dared her to stick
out her tongue
at Miss Crumb.
And she did!

One day,
Daisy's friends
thought of a really
scary dare to do.

They whispered it to Daisy.

"I'm not doing that!" she said.

"Daisy Dare-not!" they laughed.

Daisy took a deep
breath. "All right,"
she said. "I'll do it."
This was the dare:
to take the bell off
the cat's collar.

The cat was asleep. That was good.

The bell slipped off easily. That was good, too.

But Daisy's hands
trembled so much
that the bell
tinkled, the cat woke up . . .

and that was
very,
very
bad!

Daisy ran and ran
as fast as she could,
back to her friends,
through
the gate,

and into the house
where the cat
couldn't follow.

"Phew!" said Billy.
"Wow!" gasped Joe.
"You're the bravest,
most daring mouse in the whole
world!" shouted Contrary Mary.
Daisy Dare grinned with pride.
"Just dare me," she said.
"Anything you want . . .

I'm only *sometimes* scared!"